To: Madeline

MW00974924

When MUM was LITTLE

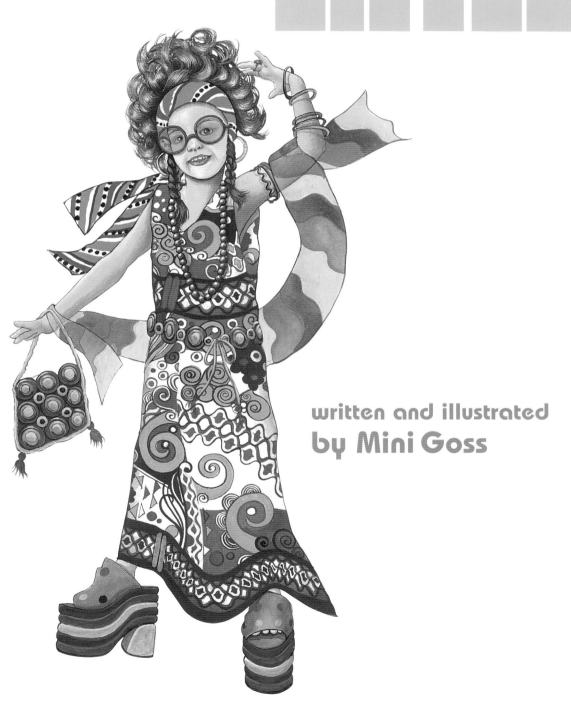

written and illustrated
by Mini Goss

Kane/Miller
BOOK PUBLISHERS

My mum wasn't always a mum.
She was little once, just like us.
That was in the olden days.
Things were different then.

Like on her seventh birthday. What do you think she got? Not a computer game. Not a CD player. They weren't even invented then. She got a pair of rollerskates.

Mum tells us *all* the time how they made their own fun.

One time her mum, our nana, was busy painting the kitchen. Mum and her brother, Rupert, collected snails from the garden and spent the afternoon painting their shells. They made a snail circus on the table — then Nana made them eat their dinner!

Mum reckons the most exciting thing that happened when she was little was that three men  were sent to the moon in a rocket. Two men got out and walked around and stuck a flag in the moon. Schools closed for the whole afternoon just so kids could see it on TV.

Mum's house was closest to the school. So everyone went there to watch.

Mum reckons that Nana was *always* going to the hairdresser. Sometimes Mum would go with her and watch all the funny looking ladies.

Mum's grandma, our great grandma, often had blue hair. Mum reckons she wanted the hairdresser to make her hair blue too. But Nana wouldn't let her.

Mum used to love watching Nana get ready to go out. If Nana hadn't been to the hairdresser for a while, she'd wear a wig. It took her ages to get ready.

Mum loves telling us how once, when Nana was all dressed up to go out, she went in and sat on Rupert's bed to say goodnight. Rupert wasn't feeling well and he vomited right into Nana's lap. Poor Nana had to get ready all over again.

Mum remembers lots of things from the olden days, even though it was so long ago.

She remembers her little sister, our Aunt Skye, being born. Mum and Rupert wanted to see the new baby but back then the doctors reckoned that kids had germs. Mum and Rupert had to stand on the lawn outside the hospital and wave to the baby.

Mum's always telling us that there was nothing like McDonald's when she was little. It was fish and chips or Chinese takeout in the olden days.

There were no plastic takeout food containers. Nana gave everyone a saucepan to put the Chinese food in. She popped the saucepans on the stove when they got home.

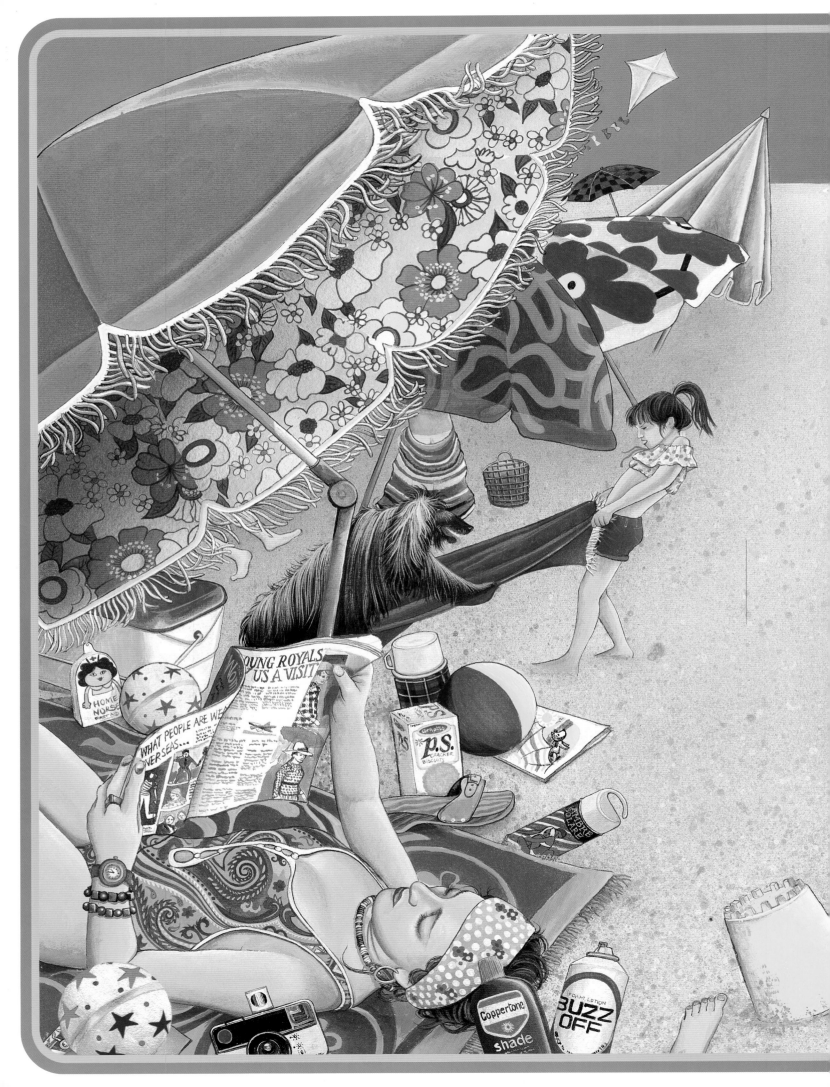

Every summer my mum's family went to the beach. One year they managed to squeeze Mum's grandma, our great grandma, into the car as well.

Mum reckons her grandma spent all day catching waves on the raft— until she lost her false teeth. She gave Rupert ten cents as a reward for finding them. It's funny to think of great grandma being a surfer.

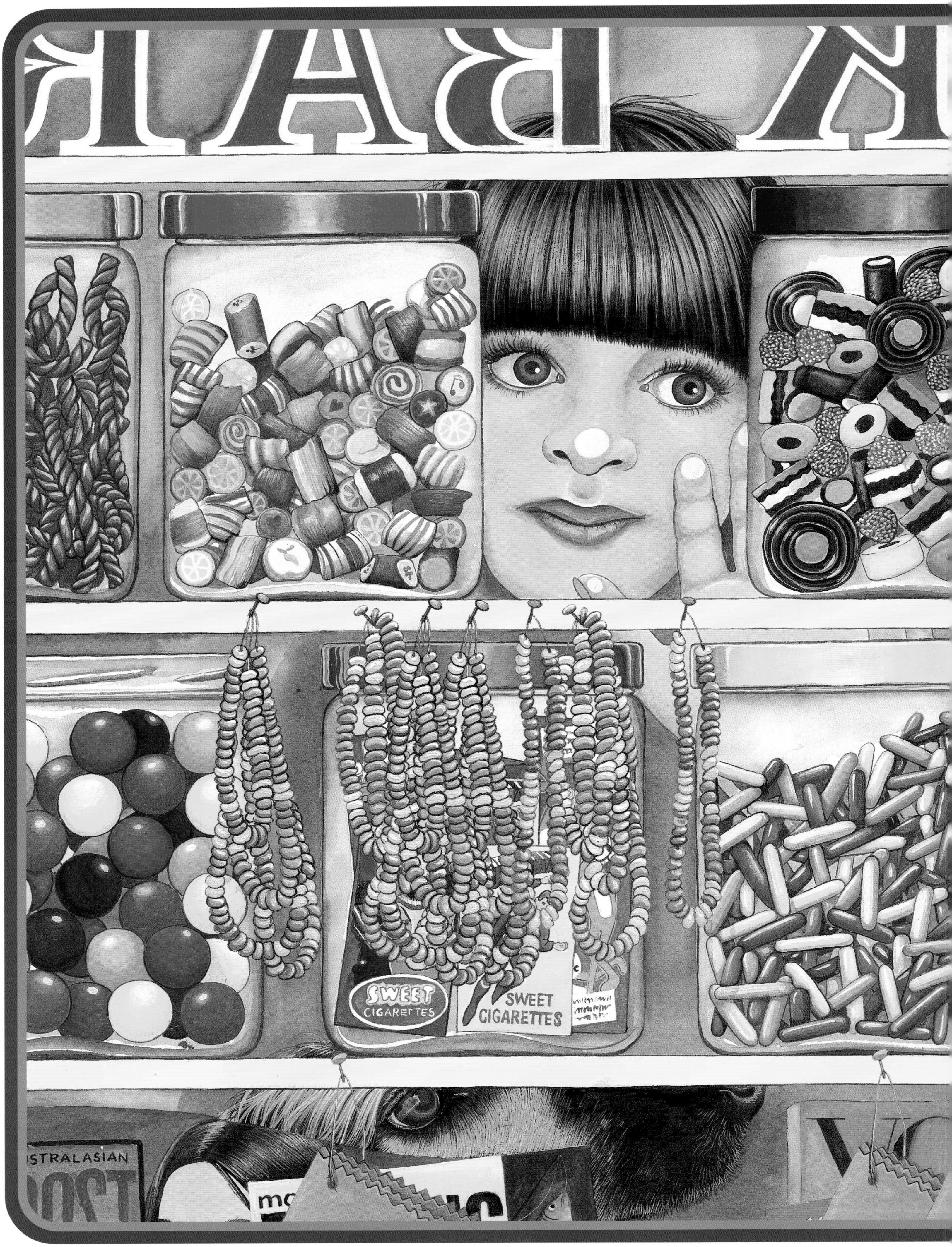
SWEET
CIGARETTES
SWEET
CIGARETTES

When Mum was little, her favorite place was the candy shop.

In the olden days, you could buy a penny's worth of this and a penny's worth of that. You could get a huge bag of candy for only ten cents. Mum says the candy was much bigger, too!

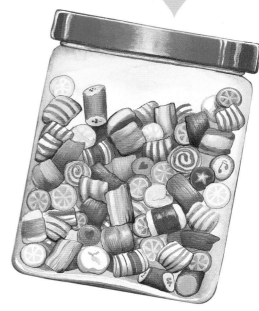

Mum always laughs when we ask her to tell us more stories about the olden days. One day, she says, you'll have your own children. And *these* days will be the olden days.

Then she says, anyway, ask your nana for some stories. She was little in ancient times.

First American edition 2004
by Kane/Miller Book Publishers, Inc.
La Jolla, California

First published in 2001 by Black Dog Books, Australia
Text and illustrations copyright © Mini Goss, 2001

All rights reserved. For information contact:
Kane/Miller Book Publishers
P.O. Box 8515
La Jolla, CA 92038
www.kanemiller.com

Library of Congress Control Number: 2004100413

Printed and bound in China by Regent Publishing Services Ltd.

1 2 3 4 5 6 7 8 9 10

ISBN 1-929132-64-6